The Blanket that Had to Go

by Nancy Evans Cooney · pictures by Diane Dawson

G.P. Putnam's Sons · New York

Text copyright © 1981 by Nancy Evans Cooney.
Illustrations copyright © 1981 by Diane Dawson.
All rights reserved. Published simultaneously in Canada
by General Publishing Co. Limited, Toronto.
Printed in the United States of America.
Library of Congress Cataloging in Publication Data
Cooney, Nancy Evans.
The blanket that had to go.
Summary: Attached to the blanket she carries everywhere,
Susi must decide what to do with it on her
first day in kindergarten since her mother
insists she shouldn't take it with her.
[1. Blankets — Fiction] I. Dawson, Diane. II. Title.
PZ7.C7843Bl 1981 [E] 79-28405
ISBN 0-399-20716-3
ISBN 0-399-21054-7 pbk.
First paperback edition published in 1984.

Fourth impression (paperback)

For Mark, with my love
and special thanks.

Susi loved her blanket. She carried it everywhere she went. The blanket was worn now, but still had its soft, warm, special smell.

Susi curled up with her blanket to
watch the cartoons on Saturday morning

or to look at her books when it rained.

She used it as a scary cape
when she was a vampire,

or as a safe raft on the
dangerous ocean of the
living room rug.

And she could always make her
brother Tommy laugh when she
became the BLUE BLOB slinking along
the floor.

Any time Susi felt tired or sick she
held a corner in her left hand and
rubbed the side of her nose with it.

And of course Susi slept with her
blanket. It was her great, good friend.

Then one warm summer day Susi and her mother went grocery shopping. When they finished loading the bags in the car, they went to buy ice cream cones.

Susi wore her blanket around
her shoulders.

Her mother said, "Susi, school starts soon. You know, in kindergarten boys and girls don't carry their blanket-friends to school with them."

Susi's tongue stopped in the middle of a chocolate-chip mint lick. No blanket!

How could she go anyplace without her blanket? It was her favorite thing in all the world. Certainly she could never start school without it.

As soon as she got home, Susi tried
to figure out a way to take the blanket
with her. She tried stuffing it into the
front of her T-shirt, but it gave her a
big, fat tummy.

She put it around her head
like a scarf, but it dragged
on the ground.

She tried to make a skirt,
but it looked funny.

She tied up her books and crayons in it for a book bag, but it still looked like a blanket.

Nothing would do. There was just no
way to take that blanket to school.

For several days Susi walked around
with a long face. Her mother couldn't
make her smile.

Tommy's tricks didn't
make her giggle.

Even her "tickle bug" father
couldn't make her laugh.

Then one day Susi's mother said, "Kindergarten starts next week." Susi still hadn't figured out what to do with her blanket friend. It was just too big to go to school.

She thought and thought. Then she
had an idea.

Susi grabbed her blanket and ran to
Tommy's room. She asked him to help
her cut her blanket in half.

The next day, when Susi's mother
took her shopping for a new school
dress, the blanket was half its size.
But it was still too big.

Two days later, when Susi went with her father to buy school shoes, the blanket was even smaller and raggedy at both ends. But it was still too big.

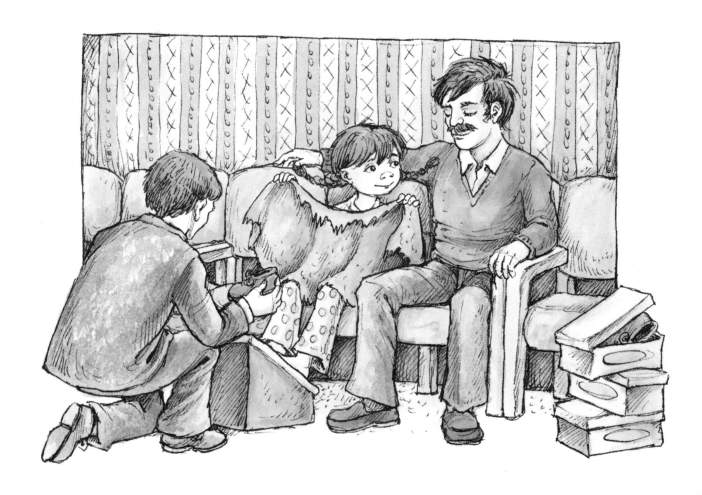

On Saturday, when she went with
Tommy to get paper and pencils, the
blanket was smaller still and jagged all
around. But it was still too big.

At last when the first day of school
came, Susi wore a smile. Her great,
good friend wasn't big enough to use as
a cape or to crawl under and become a
BLUE BLOB.

But as she set off for school she put
her hand in her pocket. There was the
blanket—only a postage-stamp piece of
blue—just the right size to go to school
with Susi.